YASMIN

The Fashionista

written by
SAADIA FARUQI

illustrated by
HATEM ALY

PICTURE WINDOW BOOKS
a capstone imprint

To Mariam for inspiring me, and
Mubashir for helping me find the
right words —S.F.

To my sister, Eman, and her amazing
girls, Jana and Kenzi —H.A.

Yasmin is published by Picture Window Books,
a Capstone Imprint
1710 Roe Crest Drive
North Mankato, Minnesota 56003
www.mycapstone.com

Text © 2019 Saadia Faruqi
Illustrations © 2019 Picture Window Books

Cataloging-in-Publication Data is available on the Library of
Congress website.

ISBN: 978-1-5158-3103-7 (hardcover)
978-1-5158-3104-4 (paperback)
978-1-5158-3105-1 (ebook pdf)

Summary: Yasmin is bored! But a glimpse of the pretty clothes in
Mama's closet turns a boring evening into a glamorous fashion
show, until, OOPS! Mama's shalwar kameez is ruined! Can
Yasmin's nani save the day before Mama gets home?

Editor: Kristen Mohn
Designer: Aruna Rangarajan

Design Elements:
Shutterstock: Art and Fashion

Printed and bound in the United States of America.
PA021

TABLE OF CONTENTS

CHAPTER 1

A New Project

Yasmin was bored. Really, really bored.

"When will Mama and Baba come home?" she asked her grandparents. "I'm tired of doing crafts. I already made three bracelets and a crown."

Nani looked up from her sewing. "They just left, Yasmin. Be patient. Surely they can have one evening out at a nice restaurant?"

Yasmin scowled. "They promised to bring me dessert. They better not forget!"

Nana held up his book.

"Come, do you want to read

some of this story with me?"

"No thanks." Yasmin shuffled

away.

She wandered into Mama and Baba's room. Something shiny caught her eye.

Yasmin crept into the huge closet. Brightly colored clothes hung from the rack. Satin kameez, silky hijabs, and beaded saris.

It was like a

rainbow swirling

around the room!

CHAPTER 2

An Accident

Yasmin couldn't help herself. She had to try on a new kameez she saw. She twirled around, arms held out, eyes closed.

"What's going on here?" Nani called out.

Yasmin looked up in surprise.

"Nani, these would look good on you!" She looped a hijab on Nani's head. She wrapped a shawl around her shoulders. "Now we're both fashionistas!"

Nani smiled. "I do look nice, don't I?"

The giggles grew louder, and the twirls grew faster, until—OOPS!

Nani stumbled. She stepped on the kameez Yasmin was wearing. Oh no! It was ripped!

Yasmin wailed, "What am I going to do?"

Yasmin took off the kameez.
Nani looked at the tear. "Don't
worry. I'll tell your mama
about it. All will be fine. I can
fix it with my sewing machine."

But the fabric was too thick. It broke the needle on the sewing machine.

"I can fix the machine," Nana said. "Just as soon as I find my glasses . . ."

CHAPTER 3

On the Red Carpet

Nana and Nani were busy

fixing the sewing machine. Mama

and Baba would be home soon.

Yasmin didn't know what to do.

She put on her pajamas.

She tidied up her craft table.

Then she got an idea.

"I know how to fix the
kameez!" Yasmin shouted. She
held up her glue gun.

Nana tried the glue gun, and
presto—it worked!

Then Yasmin had another idea. She took out the feathers and pom-poms and fabric pieces from her craft box. She cut and trimmed and taped them all onto her pajamas.

Now it was as brilliant and colorful as a peacock's tail. Just like Mama's kameez.

They heard Baba's car outside. "They're here!" Yasmin squealed. "Let's surprise them!"

When Mama and Baba entered, the room was quiet and dark. Then Nana flicked a switch. Lights! Music!

"Welcome to Yasmin's fashion show!" he boomed. "Please prepare for our fashionistas to wow you!"

Yasmin entered and struck a pose. Her pajamas shimmered. Her bangles tinkled. Then Nani joined her, modeling a colorful hijab.

Yasmin and Nani paraded

up and down the carpet, making

sure not to fall. Nani waved like a

queen.

Mama clapped her hands to

the music. Nana took pictures.

Baba yelled, "Amazing! Amazing!"

Yasmin smiled and bowed. Then she fell onto the couch between Mama and Baba. "Phew! I'm starving!" she said. "Did you bring me some dessert?"

Think About It, Talk About It

* Yasmin plays dress-up with her nani. What games or activities do you like to do with your relatives?

* Yasmin and Nani accidentally rip Mama's kameez. They fix it and plan to tell Mama when she gets home. Think about what you would do if that happened to you.

* Everyone feels bored sometimes. Make a list of five things you can try next time you feel like there's nothing to do!

Learn Urdu with Yasmin!

Yasmin's family speaks both English and Urdu. Urdu is a language from Pakistan. Maybe you already know some Urdu words!

baba (BAH-bah)—father

hijab (HEE-jahb)—scarf covering the hair

jaan (jahn)—life; a sweet nickname for a loved one

kameez (kuh-MEEZ)—long tunic or shirt

mama (MAH-mah)—mother

naan (nahn)—flatbread baked in the oven

nana (NAH-nah)—grandfather on mother's side

nani (NAH-nee)—grandmother on mother's side

salaam (sah-LAHM)—hello

sari (SAHR-ee)—dress worn by women in South Asia

Pakistan Fun Facts

Yasmin and her family are proud of their Pakistani culture. Yasmin loves to share facts about Pakistan!

Location

Pakistan is on the continent of Asia, with India on one side and Afghanistan on the other.

Capital

Islamabad is the capital, but Karachi is the largest city.

Clothing

The national dress for everyone in Pakistan is shalwar kameez. Shalwar are loose pants, and kameez is a long tunic.

Poetry

Pakistan's national poet was Allama Iqbal. He was an important person in Urdu literature.

Make a Kameez Sun Catcher

SUPPLIES:

- tracing paper or other lightweight paper
- pencil
- markers or colored pencils
- scissors

STEPS:

1. Lay the paper over this page and trace the kameez.

2. On the paper, use markers or colored pencils to create a repeating pattern along the neck, bottom, and wrists of the kameez.

3. Color the rest of the kameez using another pattern.

4. Cut out your kameez and tape to a window to make a beautiful sun catcher!

About the Author

Saadia Faruqi is a Pakistani American writer, interfaith activist, and cultural sensitivity trainer previously profiled in *O Magazine*. She is author of the adult short-story collection, *Brick Walls: Tales of Hope & Courage from Pakistan*. Her essays have been published in *Huffington Post*, *Upworthy*, and *NBC Asian America*. She resides in Houston, Texas, with her husband and children.

About the Illustrator

Hatem Aly is an Egyptian-born illustrator whose work has been featured in multiple publications worldwide. He currently lives in beautiful New Brunswick, Canada, with his wife, son, and more pets than people. When he is not dipping cookies in a cup of tea or staring at blank pieces of paper, he is usually drawing books. One of the books he illustrated is *The Inquisitor's Tale* by Adam Gidwitz, which won a Newbery Honor and other awards, despite Hatem's drawings of a farting dragon, a two-headed cat, and stinky cheese.

Join Yasmin
on all her adventures!

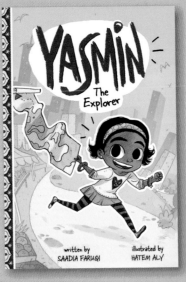

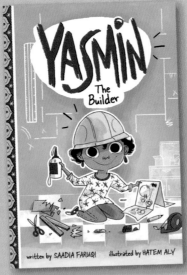

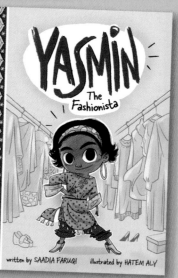

Discover more at